Colored Pencils for Lori

by

Beverly L. Moore

Illustrated by David James

outskirts press

Outskirts Press, Inc.
http://www.outskirtspress.com

ISBN: 978-1-4787-8889-8

Library of Congress Control Number: 2017913238

PRINTED IN THE UNITED STATES OF AMERICA

DEDICATIONS

To my dearest mother, Doris Alma Brown, with wishes you could be here to see how this all played out.

To the many children who feel left out and hopeless. With hopes that you truly see your way to a brighter day at the end of your rainbow.

To the memory of Mr. J. R. Effinger

Table of Contents

Chapter One

December 18, 1968

It was the last subject before the lunch bell would sound at Eldridge Park Elementary School. Lori felt pangs in her stomach, and she knew they weren't from hunger. Mr. Eddington quieted his fifth-grade class as he collected the Language Arts textbooks. Lori slowed the stream of books along her row by "accidentally" dropping Timmy's and Mary Jo's when they got to her desk. "Oops, sorry Mr. Eddington. I didn't mean to, they just slipped."

"That's okay Lori. Just speed it up so we'll have

Fireflies
Flurries
and
Funnel Cakes

enough time to get to the gifts before lunch."

This was going to be so embarrassing she thought. Lori looked around the room to see if she could cause another distraction, but found nothing that wouldn't get her into trouble and sent to the principal's office. *Maybe being sent to the principal's office wasn't such a bad idea,* Lori thought. She just had to figure out which pot of hot water she preferred to be in at the moment. Mr. Wagner would probably be in the holiday spirit and send her right back to class anyway.

Lori felt like folding up and tucking herself neatly inside one of the pages of her book. Instead she added her copy of *Fireflies, Flurries, and Funnel Cakes* to the top of the pile and handed the books to Suzanne, who stood there tapping her brand-new Buster Browns.

"Here, take these," snipped Lori. Something inside her hoped that Suzanne would just go sliding across the floor on those slippery new soles and spill the books all over the place. Lori had seen Suzanne's work displayed on the bulletin board a number of times and thought, *Not a chance! She's just too perfect.*

"Okay boys and girls, clear your desks and I'll start calling you by rows to go to your cupboards to get your exchange gifts," directed Mr. Eddington. Gleeful chatter echoed up and down the aisles. The classroom suddenly became an instant popcorn machine. Lori envisioned herself as one of those kernels that would just pop and go orbiting out onto the playground. She opened her eyes and there she was, still sitting in the middle of what would soon be one of the biggest catastrophes of her life!

Suddenly, the muffled voice of the nurse came over the intercom. "Excuse me Mr. Eddington, but could you please send Christopher Ryan to the nurse's office with his belongings? Thank you!" Without any instruction from Mr. Eddington, Christopher got up and went to his cupboard to get his belongings *and* his gift. He handed the gift to Mr. Eddington. Christopher had been anticipating this call from the nurse's office all morning. Mrs. Ryan could only schedule a twelve-thirty doctor's appointment for her son, whose congestion was only worsened by the cold weather.

"Thank you, Chris. Hope you're feeling better. Now everyone else in Chris's row, please go get your gifts."

The noise of the chairs moving away from the desks rumbled in Lori's ears like the drum section of an orchestra. Lori was terrified of drums. When she watched movies on TV, and that was when her mother's television decided to work, she always knew something terrible was about to happen. Just by the tempo of that burgeoning drumbeat. Well, this was no different. Lori knew every time a chair pulled away from a desk, truth crept in closer and closer. Soon everyone would know what they probably already suspected—that Lori and her mother were still struggling to bounce back from what had happened two years ago. By the looks of her scuffed shoes and her knotty sweater that had fuzz balls the size of "glue boogers," her classmates could see the effects of what it meant to be uprooted from the comforts of home.

"Lori, Lori. Are you listening? Your row was called," said Mr. Eddington. She had a tendency to drift off, her mind wandering, daydreaming of happier times when she and her mother lived with her grandmother. Lori was more playful back then. She had dolls, toy telephones, and even a Labrador retriever she named Blackie that would chase her from the living room into the kitchen and back every day when she'd come home. Her grandmother always had a hot meal waiting when

she and her mother arrived home after leaving the babysitter's house. Lori's mother, Alma Brown, had a pretty important job working for the county clerk down at the courthouse in the state capital. People would often tell Lori back then how smart her mother was. Lori wanted to be just like her.

The shove from Wally Smickle's foot against her chair woke Lori from her daydream. "Yes, Mr. Eddington, I heard you." Her chair slid back as slowly as she could make it go, without getting stuck on one of the floorboards. She gradually got up and scuffed her shoes against the floorboards as she went to the back of the room. In her head, she heard her father admonish, *Pick up your feet when you walk!* Lori knew she had nothing to feel proud about right then. Only proud folks picked up their feet when they walked. Somehow proud folks knew their feet were taking them someplace special. All Lori knew was that her feet were taking her toward a cupboard that didn't have a gift.

She had no gift to present. That meant there would be an *uneven exchange.* Someone would not receive something they had anticipated getting since the day after Thanksgiving break. That's when all the students picked names out of the decorated shoebox on Mr. Eddington's desk. Someone was going to be disappointed, maybe even angry. Lori did not want to make anyone upset with her. She liked it when she remained unnoticed. Lori was never one to draw attention to herself. She thought maybe if the other kids studied her too closely, they would find her flaws. To Lori, there were far too many.

She could feel the piercing looks of her classmates staring at the back of her head, through her thick ponytails. She lifted one of her arms to open the door to her cupboard. Lori felt around in her coat pockets for some change, or even a piece of candy. All she pulled out was some tissue. She scrambled around the bottom of the cupboard to stall for time. Would Mr. Eddington believe her if she told him she forgot the gift, and promised to bring it tomorrow? No. That was not going to be acceptable—Allison Stein certainly wouldn't be happy with that excuse.

Lori closed the door and left what little pride she had inside her cupboard. She turned to see what looks were coming her way as she returned to her seat. Her classmates were gazing at her in silence. No one said anything. Their silence was more deafening than the blaring sirens of the periodic emergency drill. Lori guessed it was shocking to them to see someone actually show up on the day of the exchange without a gift. Maybe *they* might have stayed home, but not Lori. Staying home was not an option. In fact, she enjoyed coming to school. For six hours, she got to escape the discomfort of what should have been the most comfortable place in the world for her.

"Class, turn around and face the front," Mr. Eddington said solemnly. It was as if he were trying to clean up the residue after a messy spill. She looked in Mr. Eddington's direction and allowed him to be her guiding light and help navigate her out of this fog of humiliation. The next row was called to go to their cupboards.

Lori sat quietly as she tried to restrain the tear that wanted to run down her face. At least a part of the burden had been lifted. She got through the walk of shame back to her desk empty-handed. Lori hoped that something like a chair would fall, or someone would sneeze. Anything that might short-circuit the silent stares around her. She wasn't going to return their baffled stares. So, she focused her attention on Edna Martin's empty chair. Edna was absent a lot, but Lori somehow knew today that Edna was probably in the same predicament as she was, and had asked to stay home.

Chapter Two

"Sofia, I believe this is for you. Come get your gift," announced Mr. Eddington. "Wee, I'm so excited! I can't wait to see what I got," screamed Sofia.

"You don't care what's inside. You're just happy to know it came from Bobby Gentry," John Brewster added his two cents. He was such a smart aleck. The other kids laughed. Lori didn't find anything funny, but just to witness someone else being ridiculed added a bit of relief to how she was feeling.

"All right, all right, that's enough. Let's continue." Mr. Eddington had a way of getting his students' attention quickly. He simply slid those thick black-framed glasses down his nose and peered over the rims with those steely eyes. Everyone quieted down and anxiously waited for the next name to be called. "Darla, this is from . . . well just come up and you'll see. I don't want any more outbursts. We have to hurry this along. I want to distribute as many of the gifts as I can before the lunch bell rings. Parker, you're next. Come up young man."

Lori lifted her head from her right hand, which had been used to prop it up. She watched Parker as he stood up from his chair and thought about how cute he looked when he smiled. His smile was enough to perk anyone up. His eyes twinkled when he flashed that future-heartbreaker smile. As he made his way to Mr. Eddington's desk, Lori watched every step. It was as if her heart was being resuscitated with each stride he took toward the front of the room.

Parker Roberts stood out with those striking good looks and he knew it. He was such a ham. He took his gift and immediately shook it, trying to figure out in his pretty head what could be inside.

"I don't think that's the way you unwrap it, Parker," joked Mr. Eddington. The class responded with its usual choreographed laughter. For the most part,

Mr. Eddington had a stern exterior, but was quite the teaser when he wanted to be. Coming from a military background, the Korean War to be exact, shaped the commanding presence he maintained in front of the class. Hearing about what he did during the war earned him the respect of his students. He relished in the responses and inquiries his war stories would conjure up. He told those stories with so much pride and courage. Lori and the others would listen closely, but Lori would listen with "extra ears on," as the old folks would say. She was a very perceptive child. She could see that Mr. Eddington needed to tell those stories to an eager audience of young, innocent, captivated listeners to help him forget some of the ugly stories about the war that he could never share with his students.

As the parade of gift recipients continued their way up to the desk, Lori wondered how Allison Stein was going to react when she didn't hear her name called. Maybe she would think her name was overlooked. Or maybe she'd put two and two together and figure out that the lifeless march that the class witnessed as Lori returned from her cupboard empty-handed had to do with the fact that it was she who was not getting a gift on this special day.

Suddenly, that dull, prolonged sound of the bell went off! That meant *everything* had to come to a halt. The class would line up and head down to the cafeteria for lunch. *Yes!* Lori thought. *Saved by the bell!* She didn't have to deal with seeing the disappointment on Allison's face when her name wasn't called, at least for now. Allison wouldn't be too happy if she didn't get a gift. *Why, of all people, did Lori have to pick* her *name?* she thought. Allison would make such a stink if she didn't get what she felt she deserved. Not to mention if she learned that her name was pulled by one of the black kids in the class. After all, Allison took every opportunity to remind her fellow classmates just how well off her family was, and what a disadvantage it was to those who could not afford a regular dose of Broadway productions like *Hair* and *Maggie Flynn* every four months. She constantly bragged about the donations her father's greeting card business made to help the poor (and everyone knew who she meant by "the poor").

The cafeteria was already buzzing when the class arrived. Lori looked up from the end of the line and thought she saw Allison, Sofia, and a few of the other girls whispering and shooting glances toward her. The only thing was, Allison didn't look too happy. Her eyes sort of narrowed when they made contact with Lori's. Lori quickly shifted her eyes in the other direction.

Tiffany, who was Lori's best friend, also noticed the glances. Lori and Tiffany had been best friends ever since that time in fourth grade when Lori stood by the bathroom door yelling to Mrs. Moore to come quick! "*She's throwing up peaches.*" Lori was afraid that her friend was going to get peach puke all over her long, straight, pretty ponytails.

"Girl, don't even pay them any mind. Don't feel bad because you didn't bring a gift. You should see what I got my person . . . My mom picked up something quick from Rexall's last night before she came home. Don't even worry about it."

Tiffany always had a way of pointing out the brighter side. Lori shook her head in agreement as she took

in her friend's comforting words. Lori gave Tiffany a big smile and even let out a sigh of relief. She didn't know how long this feeling would last, but it sure felt like good medicine for now.

"Look! They have your favorite for lunch, hot turkey sandwiches," Tiffany said with a laugh as she pointed toward the kitchen. Eldridge Park always served the good, more desirable lunches right before the holidays.

"Yeah, I could go for one of those right now, and forget about what happened earlier as I bite into one of those delicious hoagies," Lori said, her mouth watering.

Chapter Three

After dropping his class off at the cafeteria, Mr. Eddington opened the door and entered the teachers' lounge. For some reason, the room seemed a little more crowded than usual. He looked at his favorite seat and found it had already been taken by the art teacher Rose Sussman's substitute.

"Hey John, over here!" called out Barry Cole, the music teacher. "How's everything? All ready for the break? Your class gave a terrific performance at the Christmas show."

"Thank you, Barry," Mr. Eddington replied. "Yeah, I'm really looking forward to spending time with Judy and the girls. How about you?"

"Well, I have a cousin who lives up in Boston. I'm planning to go up and spend a few days. That's if we don't get any snow. I'd really like to check out the Boston Pops."

"Great orchestra! I hope for your sake that we don't get the snow," Mr. Eddington empathized. He reached into his briefcase and pulled out a crinkled brown bag. It contained the usual: an egg salad sandwich, a Gershwin pickle, and a Red Delicious apple. Mr. Eddington was a man of simple comforts. He wasn't extravagant, but rather very practical. He furnished his class in the same fashion. He supplied his students with materials that he felt would be essential for their learning, nothing more, nothing less. His wardrobe was basic too: brown Hush Puppies, brown corduroy slacks to match, topped off with gray, red, and brown plaid flannel shirts.

Mr. Cole hurriedly got up from the table. "Gotta get back and prepare a hefty stack of songs for my next class. They are quite a noisy bunch! I figure if I keep their mouths full of melodies, there will be less room for idle talking. Have a great vacation, if I don't see you!"

Mr. Eddington, lost in thought, responded, "Oh, oh you too."

Miss Philips, a bit of a busybody, noticed his behavior and asked, "Is everything all right, Mr. E? You seem miles away."

"I'm okay. It's just that I had a somewhat heart-wrenching moment in my class this morning. We were having a gift exchange before lunch, and one of my students went to her cupboard to get her gift and came back with nothing. I honestly didn't know what to say. I told the class, who was dazed and staring, to turn around and face the front. I felt so helpless."

"Who was the student? If you don't mind me asking,"

"Well, just between us, it was Lori Brown."

"I think I know her. A couple of years ago her grandmother died, and I believe she and her mother were left homeless after they lost her grandmother's house."

"Oh, I didn't realize she had all of this going on. Poor kid. How long was it before they found housing?"

"I'm not sure. Last year she and her mother had a rough time, you know, with all the adjusting. Fortunately, here at school, she had Lorna Moore in fourth grade, and you know Lorna—she's a bit of a bleeding heart. So, that helped Lori make it through that tough period," Miss Philips said as she lifted a forkful of salad. "She dodged a bullet by not being placed in Betsy Robinson's fourth-grade class. I think that might have been a lot of heartache there," she added.

"I'm really glad that you're sharing this with me. It puts a lot of things in perspective now, the acting out, the crying at the drop of a hat. I couldn't tell what was going on with her in the beginning of the school year. So, I sent her to Adam Russell for some counseling. He spends his day going around from class to class talking to students and 'picking their brains.' You know, trying to see what they want to do with their futures; but he said most of the time Lori would just sit there and ask *him* all the questions. He said he felt like she was avoiding his prodding to cover up how things really were at home. Smart kid though, turning the tables on him like that," Mr. Eddington said with a smile.

"You know what I heard?" Miss Philips said as she shifted her eyes from side to side. "I don't think there will be much joy in her home this Christmas. I hear her mother's on public assistance, and she indulges a bit . . .

if you know what I mean."

"Yeah, I sort of picked up on some of the signs I thought might be neglect. Do you know if anyone is collecting items here at school for the family?"

"Not to my knowledge. I think the concentration this year has been on students with multiple siblings; and you know that we have quite a few large families."

"Between now and the end of the school day, I have to think of something that will put a smile on that little girl's face." he pondered aloud. This is going to take some creativity on my end and you know being creative on the fly is not one of my strong suits," joked Mr. Eddington.

Chapter Four

Lori was too busy enjoying her turkey sandwich to notice the conversation taking place at the next table. She looked over at the huddle as she came up for air. In a flash her euphoria turned to angst. Suddenly, she felt this sinking feeling in the pit of her stomach. Tiffany's remedy had worn off so fast!

"Allison, what are you getting for Christmas?" Sofia inquired.

"I asked for a sterling silver charm bracelet, a pair of go-go boots, the Barbie Dream House, and a Ken doll to keep Barbie company inside her Dream House . . ." A few of the girls giggled. "I don't have to ask for the latest styles, I know they'll get them for me automatically," bragged Allison.

"Who's *they*? You mean Santa, don't you?" Timmy Myles asked in all seriousness. The entire group burst out laughing. "Hey, cut it out!" he responded as he got in the face of the boy sitting next to him. He looked back at Allison and said, "I don't know why you're laughing. You're not even getting a gift in the exchange." Just then the laughter and smiles turned to hisses and frowns.

"Where did you get that information from?" Allison asked, her interest piqued.

"Never you mind. I have my sources."

"He's a fool, Allison. Don't listen to him," Sofia answered with a scowl.

"Suppose he's telling the truth," Suzanne said cautiously. "So far, all our names from the group were called except—"

"Don't even say it!" warned Sofia.

"I sure hope I'm wrong, but we'll see when we get back from lunch." Suzanne tapped the side of her face with her index finger as she looked up at the ceiling and then toward Lori's table.

"Edna Martin's name wasn't called either," Sofia

rushed in, to spare her best friend's feelings.

"I'm not surprised. Mr. Eddington probably didn't even put her name in, knowing that she couldn't afford a gift. In my opinion, he should have left out a few other names, if you know what I mean," Suzanne hinted.

"Well if I don't get an exchange gift, someone will have a lot of explaining to do," Allison said, arrogance tingeing her words.

Lori could not ignore the fact that they were referring to her. She looked up with the meanest look on her face, and those children sitting nearby held their breath as they waited for Lori's reaction. She got to her feet and threw down what was left of her sandwich onto her tray.

"You got something to say to me? Why don't you say it to my face?" Lori shouted. The whole cafeteria became as quiet as a stuffy high-class restaurant. Lori looked around, embarrassed, as she slowly sat back down.

"Lori, I told you not to pay them any mind," reminded Tiffany. "If you're not careful, you're gonna fool around and get expelled!" Lori got up from the table, visibly upset, and ran out of the cafeteria. "See what you did? All of you need to keep your mouths shut and mind your own business!" scolded Tiffany.

"She's your friend. Why don't you go after her?" asked Suzanne. Before Tiffany could even entertain a response, she dashed out the door after Lori.

"Lori! Wait," yelled Tiffany.

"I knew this was going to happen! I knew somebody would say something to tick me off."

"Come back inside. You left your food on the table,"

"I don't want that sandwich now. Somebody probably spit on it. I don't trust any of them! Besides, if I go back in there, I know there's going to be trouble," Lori said angrily.

"When Mr. Eddington comes back to pick us up, he is going to wonder why we left the cafeteria."

"I'll just tell him I wasn't hungry. He'll understand, especially after what happened this morning."

"Well, I'm going back inside," Tiffany said hurriedly. She left Lori alone in the hallway. Lori let the first tear fall from her bowed head, and splatter onto the shiny marble floor. Then another and another, until she broke down and let loose a full-blown cascade of tears. She hadn't noticed Mr. Russell approaching from the

main office down the hall. Her hands completely covered her face. Mr. Russell knelt in front of her.

"Lori, what's the matter?" he asked gently. "Is there anything I can help you with?"

"No!" sobbed Lori. "I don't need your help. You can't help anyway."

"Did something happen? If you care to talk about it, I'm here to lend an ear," Mr. Russell assured her.

"How are you going to help me, by telling me to close my eyes and count to ten before I react?" Lori asked sarcastically.

"No, I'm not going to tell you to do that right now. First, we need to find out what's got you so upset."

"*We* need to find out? I already know what's wrong." Lori said adamantly. There it was again, that muffled annoying bell. It sounded like it was in need of repair. The closer you were to the main office, the worse it sounded. Lori could hear the students stirring, taking their trays up to dump them in the garbage. "I better go inside and remove my tray from the table," Lori insisted. Just then, Mr. Eddington appeared from around the corner.

"Hey, how's it going Mr. Russell?" Mr. Eddington

appeared a bit perplexed.

"Well, that's what I'm trying to discover from our friend here," he said as he shifted his eyes in Lori's direction.

"I know who you're talking about. I'm right here," Lori said. "I gotta go clean up my table."

"What are you doing out here anyway?" asked Mr. Eddington. Lori looked up and hesitated.

"The kids were making fun of me because I didn't bring a gift."

"So that's it!" Mr. Russell exclaimed. You would have thought he discovered a cure for the common cold.

"Yes, we had a gift exchange this morning, and I learned that Lori wasn't able to bring in a gift. Lori, let me take this opportunity without the other children around to apologize for any embarrassment you might have felt," Mr. Eddington said.

"That's okay, Mr. Eddington. It's not your fault."

"I know, but I just wanted you to know that," Mr. Eddington said, trying to comfort her. "Go back inside and line up with the class."

"Okay," Lori said as she wiped the tears from her

face. Both Mr. Eddington and Mr. Russell watched quietly as Lori went back into the cafeteria.

"I'm glad I bumped into you, because I'm at my wits' end as to what I'm going to do about this situation. You heard her, she didn't bring in a gift, which means that someone is going to get short-changed, and chances are, Lori will not have much of a Christmas this year because of the hardships her family is facing," Mr. Eddington lamented.

"I'll be quick with this, because I know you have to pick up your class . . . Simply give the gift that was designated for Lori to the student that Lori had selected, and look around the classroom for a little something that you can give to Lori that would be special to her. You must have something tucked away that you can give her so that she doesn't feel left out," Mr. Russell suggested.

At these words Mr. Eddington's mood changed and he sprang into action. "That's a great idea! Thanks so much, Adam! I will see what I have sitting around the room. I'll get back to you. See you later," he said as he and his briefcase weaved in and out of the classes that had already started making their way out of the cafeteria.

Chapter Five

As usual, Miss Philips was running late to pick up her class from the cafeteria. It was no wonder her class had a reputation for being so disorderly and disruptive; and she always appeared so frazzled, except for her perfect lipstick and eyeliner. She probably ran to the ladies' room to touch up her makeup after eating her salad and drinking her Sugar Free Tab soft drink. In any case, Lori, Tiffany, and a few of the other black children took advantage of Miss Philips's lateness by lingering at the end of Mr. Eddington's line so that they could talk to a few of the kids in Miss Philips's class.

"Hey Lori, are you okay? Who's bothering you now? Just tell us and we'll take care of them after school,"

Jody said.

"Nobody's bothering me. I just got mad about something that happened earlier," Lori answered.

"Well, you sure made a big scene for somebody who's got nobody bothering them," Jody pointed out. "Just meet us out on the playground when the bell rings. And don't have us waiting like you usually do! It's cold outside."

Every day the group discussed their plans to meet outside on the blacktop after school to walk home together. Lori could never understand the importance of mentioning it in the cafeteria *every day*, when it was an unwritten rule that that was what would happen after school. She supposed it gave the group a sense of security and consistency that sometimes went lacking in some of their lives, especially Lori's. She understood.

Things had been particularly tough at home recently. It always seemed Lori's mother had it hard around the holidays. The lights were shut off and stayed off a lot more frequently. The refrigerator always seemed emptier around this time of year. Her mother stayed out a little later each night and helped Lori less and less with her homework. No wonder she wasn't doing that well in school.

One evening last week while her mother was out, Lori decided to do a little exploring around the apartment in search of hidden Christmas gifts. She looked in the obvious places: the backroom closet, under the only bed in the apartment, and in the monstrous cabinet in the front room. All she found was a half-empty bottle of whiskey. Lori's heart dropped. She could feel all her hopes of her mother kicking the habit dissipate as she heard her mother's promises to stop drinking echo in her head. Lori quickly turned her attention and anger toward that disgusting bottle of poison. She sprang to her feet with the bottle in hand and ran over to the sink to begin the ritual of emptying the remaining contents. As she watched the alcohol cyclone its way down the drain, the brown liquid took with it all Lori's hopes and dreams of a normal childhood. Lori told herself over and over that it was not her mother's fault. Instead, she prayed for her mother. As long as this substance continued to come between her and the happiness she once shared with her mother, Lori was ready and willing to contend with this liquid enemy.

Her simple prayer went like this:

"Dear Lord, please let my mother be safe and in good health, Amen."

Lori was struck by the harsh reality that there would be no Christmas for her this year. There was not one hint of a gift anywhere around the apartment. The twenty-fifth was less than two weeks away, which left very little time for her mother to get someone to take her to downtown Trenton to do some Christmas shopping. By now her grandmother and her mom would have made sure that all the gifts were safely tucked away throughout the house. Without being noticed, Lori always managed to sneak a peek at one or two of them. The gifts were always bigger at her grandmother's house, and there always seemed to be a plentiful supply of presents under the tree on Christmas mornings back then. That was before her grandmother "went away on a long vacation" and would not be returning anytime soon. So the story went that was told to her two years ago.

"Did you bring any money for D'Amico's after school?" Jody asked.

"Lori, are you listening? Move up! The line is moving," Tiffany pushed. "Jody, Lori didn't hear you. She's a little out of it today. We'll meet you after school."

"Yeah, I can tell," Jody said as she looked Lori up and down.

"Money? No, I don't have any," Lori finally answered. Remembering how she came up empty while fishing in her coat pockets in the cupboard.

"It's too late for her to hear you now. Wake up, daydreamer!" joked Tiffany. Lori turned around and rolled her eyes at her friend. Somehow she could not get mad at her best friend. No, Tiffany made sense of a lot of things that Lori just dismissed as insignificant and unimportant. Two things Lori held sacred though, were family and home. Precisely why the nice house at the top of Maidenhead Ave. stood out to Lori. That nice house was where Tiffany and her family lived. They had rolling hills that led up to their front door.

Lori didn't know if it was some weird impulse or a curiosity to see the happenings inside of the

Washington household that triggered her bladder, but she always felt the urge to go to the bathroom every time she walked home past Tiffany's house. Mrs. Washington would always welcome Lori into her home to use the bathroom. The Washington home gave Lori feelings of comfort, happiness, and security. The house had touches of homespun traditions stamped with nostalgia. This was evident in the dishes Mrs. Washington prepared for her daughter and two sons. The homemade bread pudding and chocolate chip walnut raisin cookies made Lori's mouth water when she got whiffs of them.

About a week ago, Lori got one of her urges "to go" just as she and Tiffany came up to Tiffany's house. As Lori hobbled her way up the path to the steps, trying to restrain the flood that wanted to break through the gates, she noticed right away the markings of what appeared to be the start of a very festive Christmas season. The large fresh pine wreath on the front door ushered Lori in to what was going to be a wonderful decorative delight. Miniature houses adorned the front windows with their tiny lights aglow. A small candelabra sat on the mantel above the fireplace in the living room. She liked the way the house took her around corners in order to get from one room to the other. Unlike her mother's shotgun apartment, where everything was a straight shot from the front room to the back. Her place didn't have designated areas like the "living room" and "bedroom." Just rooms distinguished by their positioning throughout the place she had a hard time calling "home."

Chapter Six

When the class had finally settled down after lunch, Mr. Eddington asked his students if they would mind postponing exchanging the rest of the gifts until after Math. It was his call to make, but he thought it would be nice to ask anyway. He needed to review some important concepts in division before giving the class its last test before the Christmas break. He got a few objections from one side of the room. Sam Pope was the only one who found any delight in Mr. Eddington's abrupt change of plans. It was not unusual, coming from the only kid in the class who possessed the aptitude to build his own robot that could walk up and down the aisles. Lori silently harbored her own secret delight in the change of plans, but for entirely different reasons. She had hoped Mr. Eddington would just teach right up to the final bell.

"No fair, Mr. Eddington," objected Allison. "You see, some of us are anxiously waiting to be called up to get our gifts. Now we must remain in suspense until the end of the day."

"A little bit of suspense never hurt anybody. It keeps life interesting," said Mr. Eddington. "Stop complaining and take a look at the word problems on the board. You are going to see some on the test tomorrow. Can I get a volunteer to read the first one aloud?" Mr. Eddington wiped the chalk dust on his hands onto his corduroy pants as he waited for a response. Parker finally raised his hand. "Parker, you never disappoint. Thank you."

"Jenny's mother made three dozen cupcakes for her class of eighteen students. How many cupcakes does each student get?" Parker recited proudly.

"Very nice job, Parker," complimented Mr. Eddington. "What is the first thing we must determine?"

"First, we have to determine how many cupcakes make up three dozen," answered Sam.

"Good start. What is the next step?"

"Then . . ." continued Sam.

"That's enough for now, Sam. Let's give someone else a chance. Mary Jo, do you wanna give it a shot?"

"Not really, Mr. Eddington," Mary Jo said shyly. She blew a big bubble that splattered all over her face. The class started laughing. *That must have taken at least two pieces of Bazooka to blow a bubble that big*, Lori thought. The sight of that bubble took Lori back to the spring afternoons she and Mary Jo would sneak across the street to Mr. Herman's store to buy Bazooka gum for a penny apiece. Lori was not allowed to go past the end of the fence that kept the horses in. Mary Jo's family lives near the house Lori's grandparents owned. They have four beautiful horses that graze inside a fenced-in property. She and Mary Jo would climb the fence and call to the horses. Mary Jo knew each horse by name. Lori would hold on to the fence and watch as Mary Jo blew large bubbles that would pop in the spring breeze and cover her mouth and nose.

"Okay, spit that gum out right now Mary Jo! Lori, why don't you help us out," asked Mr. Eddington. A slight murmur rippled on one side of the room.

"I don't know how that's possible . . . ," Suzanne said under her breath, "if someone can't figure out that gifts cannot be evenly divided if they fail to bring theirs in." Suzanne's clique snickered loud enough for Mr. Eddington and the rest of the class to hear.

"That's enough!" he yelled. "This is no longer funny. I want this ridicule to stop here and now! Or no one will be taking home presents. Lori, you don't have to answer if you don't want to," he said as he looked in her direction. She had already retreated. Her head was down and the class could hear some soft sobbing. Some of the children looked disgustedly in Suzanne's direction, who showed a bit of remorse for her mean words. "I want everyone to take out their binders. Open to a clean page and write the two word problems down and solve them on your own. When you get the answers, I want you to sit there quietly. Do not share your answers with your neighbor. If I hear any talking, it's an automatic five points deducted from your test tomorrow," Mr. Eddington said rather sternly.

The room immediately went into a silent lockdown. The students busily worked on the math problems. Lori raised her hand to ask if she could be excused to go to the bathroom. Mr. Eddington allowed a couple of other girls in Lori's row to go with her. When they quietly exited, Mr. Eddington used the time to follow Mr. Russell's advice about searching around the room for something special to present to Lori, who had suffered enough wounds for one day. He made his way to the closet at the back. In a box at the bottom was a container labeled LOST AND FOUND. Mr. Eddington rummaged around with his large hands, not finding the right item. Besides, he didn't want to mistakenly give her something that belonged to one of the other children—God forbid! He soon discovered that there was not much in the closet of any value except for the few valuables that belonged to others. That was a can of worms he did not prefer to open on this day.

The floorboards creaked under the tread of Mr. Eddington's steps as he made his way back to the front of the room. A few arms rose with questions as he went by. Once he addressed them, Mr. Eddington continued on his quest. He pulled out a couple of drawers in his large desk. The class could tell those bottom drawers weren't used to being opened and closed. They got stuck and he had a hard time pulling them open. He knew there was nothing in them that would put a smile on the face of a ten-year-old girl, yet he searched anyway. He came across a copy of last year's *Farmers' Almanac* and Flora Durham's bat and ball he confiscated earlier in the school year.There was one last place he had not checked, but by that time the girls had returned from the lavatory, and a couple of fast workers had already finished the word problems.

"All right, girls from Sofia's row, you may go use the lavatory. I want you to come right back. We have others who are waiting to use the lavatory," Mr. Eddington reminded them. While the class prima donnas were out of the room, Mr. Eddington took this opportunity to check on Lori. "Hey kid, how are you doing?"

"I'll be okay, but right now I just want this day to end so I can get out of here and go home."

"How are things at home, Lori?"

Lori looked surprised that Mr. Eddington was asking about her life outside school. Lori was always a little cautious and protective when it came to talking about how things were with her and her mother. She looked around to see if anyone was listening. She couldn't help but notice the class busybody, Nora Tinsley, peering over her thick glasses in their direction. By now, she had finished her work and had opened her diary. The last thing Lori needed was to be the headline of the day in Nora's diary!

"What are you staring at?" Lori sneered at Nora. Nora got so nervous that when she slammed her diary shut, she sent pages from it flying as it dropped on the floor. Nora was already the nervous type who couldn't manage to get through a day at school without being the brunt of some cruel prank. Lori momentarily gained some strength at the price of Nora's feebleness.

"She's harmless. Leave her be, Lori. Right now, I'm more concerned about you," Mr. Eddington said, redirecting his attention back to Lori.

"I already told you that you don't have to worry about me, Mr. Eddington. There's nothing you can do to help me," Lori said defensively.

"Well, maybe I can help. If there's a way I can make up for the embarrassment you experienced today, I'm willing to do it," Mr. Eddington offered. Lori looked up at him with puffy eyes that were now reddened from tears.

"I know I haven't been the most well-behaved

student and I'm sorry for the way I may have acted...," she said with sincerity. She was halted by a show of emotion when tears started to well up in her eyes again for the umpteenth time today. Mr. Eddington handed her a tissue from the box on his desk. She continued: "My mother and I had to move from our house where we lived when my grandmother was alive. To this day, no one in the family has told me what *really* happened to my grandmother. They all stick to their stories that she went away on some sort of vacation and will not be back for a long time. My mother said she went to Florida. My aunt said she went to Alabama. I'm no baby. I know when someone has been gone as long as she has, they must not still be living. My grandmother would not have just left us alone in the house like that, knowing how much my mother and I needed her."

Mr. Eddington gave her a light pat on the shoulder. "I accept your apology. Don't worry, I understand how difficult it is to lose someone you love," he sympathized. Lori gave the most genuine smile that she had given in a long while.

Chapter Seven

The clock on the wall read 1:38 PM. Mr. Eddington had just wrapped up the math review by giving the class the answer to the first word problem. "You divide eighteen into thirty-six, because thirty-six is the number of cupcakes that you have to split among eighteen students. How many times will thirty-six cupcakes go around among eighteen students?"

"Two times!" called out Billy Carter.

"That's correct, Billy. Next time raise your hand, though," Mr. Eddington gently reminded him. Billy simply beamed with pride, knowing that he got an answer right—before the whole class. He heard Mr. Eddington's advice, but he wasn't letting the opportunity to show his intelligence slip by. "A show of hands, how many of you copied and solved the second word problem?" Five hands went up. "The rest of you will solve it for homework. Make sure you have it copied down before you leave today. We will move on to the rest of the gifts, but before I start, let me say this. . ." Mr. Eddington paused."Everyone will leave here with something today, despite what you may have heard. Although, I must warn you, if I hear one snicker, or one snide remark about *ANYTHING*, everyone is going to give back their gift to the person who brought it in, and you're all going home with the gifts you came in with! Understood?"

"Yes," chimed the class in concert.

"Okay, we will continue with the next name," Mr. Eddington said as he lifted a nice-sized box. "Kimberly Bennett. Boy, this is big! I wonder what it is, a set of pots and pans?" Mr. Eddington said jokingly. His humor made tense moments seem light. "Next we'll call up Allison Stein." She sat up with such surprise that she nearly propelled herself to the front of the room as she sprang to her feet. There was a hushed gasp from her section as she approached the front and extended her hands to receive her gift.

Mr. Eddington had quietly gone through the presents earlier as the students were working on their word problems. He inconspicuously wrote Allison's name on a piece of paper and taped it to a rectangular box in red gift wrap, sprinkled with little Christmas trees. While he held the gift in his hand, he felt a slight tinge of guilt. Inside was something that had been specifically picked out for Lori.

Mr. Eddington imagined that when Simon Lange went with his mother to pick out the present, he knew exactly the right gift that would put a smile on Lori's face. Simon probably deliberated carefully before making his selection. Mr. Eddington had a knack for watching his students when they thought he wasn't looking. Many times, he'd noticed Simon staring at Lori as she did her work. Mr. Eddington saw the way Simon went in such a roundabout way around the room to sharpen his pencil. He figured Simon must have a healthy schoolboy crush on Lori. It's not as if Lori hadn't noticed Simon's peculiar ways, she had. She felt kind of special that her homely appearance caught the attention of this blond-haired German kid. She occasionally returned his glances with a smile. She would even go out of her way to sit by him in the music room. Two shy kids sharing a bit of puppy love. Lori savored the attention she got from Simon at school, because she knew nothing would come of it beyond the four walls.

Mr. Eddington felt like somewhat of a spoiler in this romance. Here he was at the precipice of altering the path of Cupid's arrow, and he felt sorry for doing so, but there was a more immediate crisis at hand. Switching the name tag for this handwritten piece of paper needed to be done in order to keep the peace and avoid a calamity. He would make it up to Lori, he promised himself.

Chapter Eight

Allison held on to the gift as if she had stumbled onto the key to some hidden treasure. Though it was small in comparison to what she was accustomed to receiving, this didn't matter to her. Not after coming so close to not receiving anything at all, she thought. She humbly accepted the small token and drew it to her heart in a forged attempt to show how deeply she cherished it. She smiled and proudly took her seat. Allison barely touched her chair before her friends swarmed around her. "Let's see, let's see! Open it," they urged.

"Hold on. Wait a minute!" shouted Allison. She delicately peeled the ends of the wrapping first, as she was probably taught in her etiquette classes. The others in her circle could not take the suspense as they hovered like vultures. Now she was working her way along the edges of the long rectangle.

Simon really had not paid much attention to the swap that had taken place. He was too busy watching Lori's every move. He knew she was having a rough day. All the more reason to get his gift in her hands to hopefully cheer her up. He didn't even notice that his remedy for Lori's ills had fallen into the hands of another.

A loud chorus of oohs and ahs came from Allison's side of the room. She took her gift and released a spray that seemingly hypnotized those within a certain radius. The girls all had their eyes closed as they pointed their noses up to inhale the sweet-smelling fragrance. Seeing the delight on her friends' faces, Allison turned around in her chair in Simon's direction and squealed across the room, "Oh Simon, you didn't have to, but I understand that you had to go all out to satisfy my fancy taste." He gave her a befuddled look.

"Why, why I . . . ," Simon stuttered.

Suddenly, Mr. Eddington made a loud clearing sound in his throat. "Class, we will finish the gift exchange with the last few names. Tiffany, will you come up next?" She looked over in Lori's direction as she got up. Lori gave her a slight smile. Tiffany thanked Mr. Eddington as he handed her the gift.

Buddy Davis sang a line from Stevie Wonder's "I Was Made to Love Her" to signal to Tiffany that it was his gift that she had accepted. Tiffany looked in his direction and gave a nervous laugh as she took her seat. Her desk was in the row next to Lori's. Tiffany sensed Lori's uneasiness when she heard her breathing heavily and saw Lori squirming out of the corner of her eye.

"Relax Lori," Tiffany said to set her friend at ease. "If you get called, just act normal and go up there like nothing happened."

"That's easy for you to say. You already went, and besides . . . you *brought* a gift," Lori snapped back. She continued showing signs of nervousness. By now, the jitters moved down to her feet; she was wildly tapping her shoes.

"Will you stop it? You're starting to draw attention," Tiffany pleaded. Several kids nearby began to dart their eyes in Lori's direction. At this point, it didn't matter anymore to Lori what the other students thought. She knew she would be facing her moment of truth sooner rather than later.

Just then there was a knock at the door. Mr. Eddington went over to open it to see who it was. He found Mr. Russell standing in the doorway looking a bit out of sorts.

“Why don’t you come in, Mr. Russell,” Mr. Eddington said.

“Thank you, John. Um...I took the liberty of making a phone call, or quite a few that is, until I got in touch with...Miss Brown,” Mr. Russell said quietly with some hesitation. “I thought she should know what was happening with Lori.”

“So, what did she say? She wasn’t upset, I hope.”

“Well, she wasn’t too happy to know that we found out just how difficult things have been at home. She said she felt we were ‘meddling’ in her business,” Mr. Russell noted. “After I let her vent, she started feeling bad that she was the cause of Lori’s embarrassment today, and said she wanted to come in.”

“She’s here in the building? Where?” Mr. Eddington said, his face full of surprise.

“Yes, I told her to wait in the main office until I

came to get you."

"Me, she wants to talk to me? What about?" Mr. Eddington sounded a little agitated. "Aww, come on Adam, I'm in the middle of the gift exchange. I'd like to finish up before dismissal."

"I can't think of anyone other than you who is equipped to fill her in," Mr. Russell answered. "So, why don't you go down to the main office while I stay here and watch your class?" Mr. Eddington bit his bottom lip in frustration, but reluctantly edged his way out the door.

"I'll be back shortly, everyone. Mr. Russell is staying with you until I get back. I don't want anyone giving him any problems. Remember what I said about those gifts you have," he warned.

"We'll be good, Mr. Eddington," Wally Smickle promised. He followed his remark with a smirk as he gave his buddy Alan Gibson a glance.

"I'll handle things from here, Mr. Eddington," Mr. Russell said firmly as he stared in Wally's direction. Wally retreated quietly, sliding his long legs out from under the desk as he slouched in his chair. Another plot to gain attention foiled again.

Mr. Eddington didn't really want to hurry to the main

office to face the confrontation that awaited him, but at the same time he knew he had to in order to get back to his class in time to finish giving out the gifts. He envisioned the disappointed look on the faces of the students who had yet to be called up. He held his breath, yanked at the doorknob, and stepped inside the main office. He caught Mr. Wagner's attention just as he finished speaking with his secretary, Mrs. O'Brien.

"Hi, John. Come right in. I believe Miss Brown would like to speak with you," he said as he directed Mr. Eddington toward his office. "Have a seat, Mr. Eddington. I believe you know Miss Brown, Lori's mother."

"Yes, we met once before during a parent-teacher conference," Mr. Eddington affirmed. Miss Brown acknowledged his recollection with a slight nod.

"Hello, Mr. Eddington," Miss Brown said as she looked up from her lap. Sitting in the principal's office with her child's teacher was one of the *last* places she wanted to be.

"As you may know by now, Mr. Russell contacted Lori's mother to let her know about an incident outside the cafeteria. He consulted with me and I gave him the go ahead to make the call. I felt that it was the right thing to do," explained Mr. Wagner. Miss Brown seemingly nodded in agreement.

"Yes, I understand, and I'm glad you took the time to come in today," Mr. Eddington replied. "I was very troubled by the incident myself. I wish we didn't have to put Lori or you through any embarrassment. I am truly sorry for that."

"Yes, I'm sorry too," Miss Brown replied. "Lori is a very sensitive child and the slightest thing can upset her. I hope she did not cause a disruption in your class, Mr. Eddington. I must say that between you and Mrs. Moore last year, the two of you have worked with Lori so much and I really do appreciate it."

"No, don't worry. Lori is not a problem. Despite the situation, she handled herself fairly well," Mr. Eddington assured her. Miss Brown seemed a little less tense at those words. "I'd like to know what it is that I can help you with today," asked Mr. Eddington.

"Well, when I got the message that Mr. Russell had called, I thought it was some kind of emergency or something. Then I called the school back to see what was going on. He explained something about Lori being upset because she did not have a gift to bring to school. She did not tell me she needed a gift until last night." Mr. Wagner sighed at Miss Brown's explanation. "It's the truth!" Miss Brown exclaimed. "Lori is so silent about a lot of things at times. I don't know how to get her out of that."

"How can we help out, Miss Brown?" Mr. Wagner asked.

"Maybe you've done enough already. I don't want the school getting any more involved than it needs to right now," she said, her tone slightly annoyed.

"Mr. Russell did say you weren't too happy to find out that the school was aware of your current situation. But you have to understand that the school plays a very important role in the day to day of your child's life," Mr. Wagner explained.

"I do realize that, but I just wish the school would also be respectful of boundaries. You should not always go sticking your nose where it doesn't belong." Miss Brown's anger was starting to more clearly surface. Mr. Eddington was beginning to fidget in his chair. Mr. Wagner moved the microphone on his desk to get an unobstructed view of Miss Brown.

"Now wait a minute. Let me explain a couple of things," Mr. Wagner responded. "Once you release your daughter into our care each day, her well-being becomes our responsibility. And if that means trying to find out from your daughter what is bothering her, then that is what we will attempt to do. It is difficult for a child who is burdened to properly learn." His words seemed to strike a chord. Miss Brown softened her disposition a bit, and shifted in her chair.

"Yes, I know you're supposed to do all that you can to help my child, but some things need to be left to the family to figure out," Miss Brown responded, sharpness in her tone. "We've been going through some adjustments since my mother died a couple of years ago, but we have a place now. I haven't found work yet, so that has been hard. This time of year *especially* is the worst time to be broke."

"Yes, I am aware of what you've been going through, Miss Brown. As the principal said, if there's any way we can help you and Lori out, please let us know," Mr. Eddington reassured her. "Look, I don't mean to rush this, but I promised the kids I would come back soon to finish up the gift exchange."

“We will wrap this up, but before you go, I believe Miss Brown has something that she brought with her that she would like to give you to help make up for the gift mix-up,” Mr. Wagner pointed out.

“I don’t want to take up much more of your time, but let me say a couple of things,” Miss Brown said. “It may not show at the moment, but I really do appreciate you offering to help; and maybe there is something you can do. As I said, I have not been able to find work and it’s been tough just trying to pay rent, keep the lights on, and put food on the table, let alone having any spare money to buy gifts for Christmas,” she admitted. “I hate to ask, but . . . if the school has any toys or something small, doesn’t have to be anything big . . . I would certainly appreciate you pitching in.”

“I’m sure we can find something in the collection that the teachers have gathered,” Mr. Wagner said. Mr. Eddington looked at him a bit puzzled, because he was told that the collection had already been designated for distribution to the families with many children. Lori was an only child.

“I will look into that by talking to Miss Philips. See what we can do,” Mr. Eddington said as he rose to his feet. He extended his hand to shake Miss Brown's, but she reached down beside the chair where she was sitting.

"When I found out how not having a gift to give made Lori feel, I felt ashamed," Miss Brown said. "I had to do something. I couldn't let my baby feel left out. I know that must have been horrible for her. May I go to your classroom to see her?"

"School will be over in about forty minutes. You'll have plenty of time this afternoon to check on her," Mr. Wagner said.

"Well, the first thing I'm going to do is give her the biggest hug. May I at least leave these candy canes with you to give to her so that she'll have a little something to pass out to the children?" she asked as she pulled two boxes of candy canes from a plastic bag. Mr. Eddington was pleasantly surprised. He had not expected this; and he knew Lori would be surprised, too. "I asked my neighbor if he could take me to McCrory's before coming here. It was a sacrifice to spend the little bit of money that I do have on these boxes, but I think having these candy canes to give out is just what Lori needs at the moment."

"That was nice of you. I'm sure this is going to make Lori feel extra special," Mr. Eddington said with a smile as he reached for the boxes. He tucked them under his arm, and once again, extended his hand to shake Miss Brown's. This time his hand met hers with an enthusiastic grasp. "Thank you for the candy canes and for taking the time to come in."

"You're welcome, and I'm sorry for any misunderstanding," she apologized.

"No need to feel bad. I believe you have come to the rescue at just the right time!" Mr. Eddington's eyebrows rose a little as he thought of just the perfect present to give to Lori. He gleamed with satisfaction in knowing that her mother's seemingly small gesture would restore the dignity her daughter had lost when she looked in that cupboard.

Chapter Nine

His feet were just not taking him down that long hallway fast enough. With each step, it became clearer to him what he could give Lori for Christmas. It wasn't until Miss Brown handed him the candy canes that he remembered he had a box of colored pencils that he never opened when the students were working on their science projects back in October. Certainly those would perk her up. *I believe she likes drawing pictures, so colored pencils would be perfect,* he thought. Mr. Eddington had gotten so excited just thinking about the turnaround of events that was about to take place that he almost dropped the candy canes as he opened the door to his classroom. *What a mess that would have been!* he thought.

"He did too!" yelled Sofia. Mr. Eddington stepped into what appeared to be the Battle at Bunker Hill. Mr. Russell had made little progress in getting the two sides to resolve their dispute.

"All right, settle down!" Mr. Eddington ordered. "We don't have a lot of time left, and I still have things to do before we end the day. Thank you for supervising the class, Mr. Russell. I'll fill you in tomorrow," he whispered as Mr. Russell exited the room. "Now, I hope you guys didn't embarrass me with that little episode that was taking place."

"You'll read all about it in my next newsletter, Mr. Eddington," Nora reported. Some of the children scowled and growled in her direction while others thought it was funny and laughed rather loudly.

"Thank you, Nora. I'm sure it'll be very entertaining. But let's get back to the gift exchange." Mr. Eddington went through the remaining names as though he were trying to rush through the main course to get to dessert.

Some of the students couldn't help but notice that a certain student's name was not called to come up and get a gift. They glanced over in Lori's direction to see her reaction. Many of their faces wore the same expressions they had earlier in the day when Lori went straight to her seat instead of going up to Mr. Eddington to hand him her gift. Even Allison's friends felt a bit sorry for how they had been treating her that day. Lori knew her classmates were watching to see how she was handling the situation, how she was managing to hold herself together. *No more tears*, Lori thought. Besides, she had cried enough for one day. Soon she'll be home and tomorrow will be another day. Finally, Tiffany's advice was sinking in.

"And now, I have a surprise for you. Lori, will you please come up here. Your mother dropped these off at the main office. She said you were in such a rush to get to school that you left these on the table," Mr. Eddington said as he revealed the bright red and white sticks of savory peppermint and sugar.

"Ooh" resounded up and down the aisles as Lori slowly got up from her chair. She was just as surprised as the other children. The vivid stripes of red and white

gleaming through the plastic covering the boxes resembled a lighthouse Lori once saw on a calendar, a glowing beacon in the deep darkness where the ocean meets the sky at night. Lori saw the candy canes as that lighthouse. She beamed with joy as she made her way to the front of the room.

"Here Lori, why don't you open the boxes and pass the candy canes out to the class," Mr. Eddington suggested. "To make the process go a little quicker, why don't you call someone up to help you." Hands went up all over the room.

"Pick me, pick me," came from every corner of the room. Tiffany would have been the obvious choice, but Lori felt that she owed a small favor to someone else in the class.

"I pick Allison to help me," Lori said. Allison put her hand down and proudly came up to the front, happy that she had been selected. Lori smiled proudly as she handed the second box to Allison. Lori hadn't felt this much pride in a long time.

"You take one side of the room Lori, and Allison, you take the other," directed Mr. Eddington. Each girl walked up and down the aisles, delicately placing the

candy canes on each student's desk so that none would be broken.

While the girls were busily attending to their duty, Mr. Eddington slipped to the side of the room where the large supply closet was located. He carefully searched it, without drawing attention from the children. Bingo! he whispered under his breath.

He found what he was looking for. There they were, a fresh box of Eberhard Faber colored pencils. All of which had been pre-sharpened to pinpoint perfection. Mr. Eddington secured them tightly in his grasp. He removed the box from the closet as if it were gold in Fort Knox. He somehow knew the value these pencils would have for the little girl who would come to possess them.

Once the girls completed their task, Mr. Eddington had one additional request. "Since it is late in the day, and I don't want anyone running outside with a candy cane sticking out of their mouths, I want you to wait until you get home before you open them. Better yet, hang them on your trees at home." The class just responded with snickers and mischievous giggles. He knew as well as they did that those plastic wrappers would be peeled off the minute they hit the playground.

It was now 2:40 PM, twenty minutes before the bell would ring for dismissal. Mr. Eddington did not know just how he was going to handle presenting the colored pencils to Lori. This would be a bit trickier than he anticipated. Should he call her up in front of the whole class? Would that embarrass her? Should he secretly slip the box in her little briefcase? He stood there and contemplated how he would feel if he were in the same situation. That's something they drummed over and over to the teachers in one of their meetings: "You should put yourselves in the students' shoes. Feel how they would feel, and ask yourselves . . ." Right now, Mr. Eddington was asking himself a few questions that he did not know the answers to.

Chapter Ten

He looked around the room and immediately noticed the positive reaction created by the candy canes. Lori was like a new person compared to earlier in the day. She was bubbly now, engaged in conversations with children who she never had more than two words to say to before today. Should he interrupt the interactions going on before him? In fact, the entire class looked like the closing ceremony of a roundtable at the United Nations. Maybe now would be a good time to interject. Use the box of colored pencils as a lesson on differences, just like the differences at the UN. "Boys and girls, may I have your attention? As I look around, I see something wonderful happening.

I'm reminded of the lesson on the United Nations that we learned back in October. There are conversations taking place between individuals who never spoke to each other before. It just warms my heart; and to think, all over that whimsical treat called the candy cane."

"No need getting all mushy, Mr. Eddington," Parker said bashfully.

"The United Nations is a meeting of minds between the leaders of some of the most powerful countries in the world. I look at each one of you as future leaders someday. Some of you will become doctors, lawyers, and perhaps some of you will become teachers like yours truly."

"Who's yours truly, sir?" asked Timmy. The girls in the class couldn't help but giggle at his absurd question.

"Timmy, it's just an expression, a figure of speech."

"Oh, I knew that all the time, Mr. Eddington," Timmy said, recovering nicely.

"As I was saying, this classroom represents the UN right now. I'm holding a box of colored pencils, which in a sense is as different as those leaders at the UN."

"Mr. Eddington, what is this, another lesson on the United Nations?" Parker asked. "We already did that unit, we remember what you taught us."

"Parker, don't interrupt me. This box of pencils represents the United Nations. If I recall correctly, we have a day on the calendar designated as United Nations Day." Mr. Eddington weaved his web nicely. "Who can tell me what day we celebrate United Nations Day?" Almost effortlessly, without much thought, a hand shot up immediately on the right side of the classroom. "Yes, Lori. Can you answer the question?"

"October twenty-fourth!" she said proudly. "I know because that's my birthday!"

"You are absolutely right," said Mr. Eddington. "Will you come up and get this beautiful box of colored pencils since you answered correctly?" This was turning out to be a very lucky day for Lori. First, her mother came through by bringing in the candy canes, and now she had just won herself a brand-new box of colored pencils (so she thought). She marched to the front of the class again. Mr. Eddington gave her one of his biggest smiles along with the box of colored pencils. He was relieved to have figured out a way to get the

pencils in the hands of such a deserving child. As Lori reached up to take possession of the colored pencils, Mr. Eddington bent down and whispered in her ear, "By the way, Merry Christmas Lori."

The End

Acknowledgements

It is with sincere gratitude that I first acknowledge God for the gift of writing my first book *Colored Pencils for Lori*, that hopefully will be shared by many. Reverend Dr. James A. Kuykendall prophesied that I would write books. I thank you for the courage to speak those words many years ago. I thank my sister in law, Kathy Nelson Moore for inviting me to speak at her school. Through this invitation, I was led (not by chance) to reveal an incident in my childhood to those students at School #12 in Paterson, NJ., which blossomed into this heart-warming story. I thank my skilled and resourceful goddaughter, Alysha Bullock for her guidance in the early stages of the book. To my best friend,

Bettina Bullock (Tiffany), who believed in the story and encouraged me in my journey. To my illustrator, David James whose artistic talent captured the images I was looking for. To the students at Don Bosco Technology Academy, thank you for your instincts and feedback. A special thanks to the place where *Colored Pencils for Lori* originated, the Eldridge Park Elementary School of the Lawrence Township Public Schools district. To the school's principal, Ms. Robbins for allowing me access to further research my book. Thank you, Kathy Carter for helping me architect a plan for success with my book. Drawing from your own personal experiences proved very helpful! To Dominick Montalto for your editing expertise. To Colleen Goulet for your support, guidance, and words of comfort during this process. To Chuckie and Gloria Batchelor, you certainly work together great as a team in your efforts to package the perfect picture. Last, but certainly not least, my family. To my husband, Brian, even through your health challenge, your courage demonstrated that according to our son, "Your heart was way bigger than that pillow!" To my daughter, Yolanda, whose real emotions [after reading the book] confirmed to me that this story is one which should be shared with others. To my son, David, your style and wit continue to make me proud. I have gained strength and encouragement from all of you! For that, I'll be forever grateful.

CPSIA information can be obtained
at www.ICGtesting.com
Printed in the USA
BVOW06s0443220118
505928BV00001B/2/P